A First Flight® Level Three Reader

Ellen's Terrible TV Troubles

By
Rachna Gilmore

Illustrated
by John Mardon

Fitzhenry & Whiteside • Toronto

Text Copyright © 1999 by Rachna Gilmore
Illustration Copyright © 1999 by John Mardon

First published in the United States in 2000.

Fitzhenry & Whiteside acknowledges with thanks the support of the Government of
Canada through its Book Publishing Industry Development Program in the publication of this title.

Printed in Hong Kong.
Cover and book design by Wycliffe Smith Design.

10 9 8 7 6 5 4 3 2 1

Canadian Cataloguing in Publication Data
Gilmore, Rachna, 1953-
Ellen's Terrible TV Troubles

(A first flight level three reader)
"First flight books"
ISBN 1-55041-525-5 (bound)
ISBN 1-55041-527-1 (pbk.)

I. Mardon, John   II.Series: First flight reader.

PS8563.I57E44 1999a   jC813'.54   C99-931307-X
PZ7.G43805EI 1999

For my friend, Tina

R.G.

For Judy,

J.M.

CHAPTER ONE

Ellen was watching her favourite
Saturday morning cartoon show. All
of a sudden, the TV made a strange
hiccuping sound and went blank.

"Hey!" cried Ellen. She fiddled the
dials but nothing happened.

Her father and mother even shook
the TV, but still nothing happened.

"We'll get it fixed Monday," said Ellen's mother.

"Monday!" screeched Ellen. "That's two whole days!"

"Never mind. It's a lovely day," said Ellen's father. "Let's go out and enjoy the sun."

"No thanks," said Ellen, scowling.

After her parents left, Ellen thumped the TV again. Nothing.

CHAPTER TWO

Ellen closed her eyes and took a deep breath. With all her might she wished, "Please, please, please, please, PLEASE! I want the TV to work in my living room."

She heard a soft burping sound from the TV.

Ellen opened her eyes. Crossing her fingers and toes, she reached for the remote control. She pressed the on button.

It worked! There were her favourite cartoon characters chasing each other across the screen.

"I did it!" cried Ellen. With a big grin, she sat down to watch.

A cartoon dog was chasing a blue cat. Ellen laughed. The dog was getting closer and closer. It snarled at the cat.

The cat looked over its shoulder. It yowled and leaped — out of the TV, straight towards Ellen.

Ellen jumped to her feet. The cat flashed between her legs and ran up the lampshade. The dog came snapping after it.

The cat screeched and disappeared around the corner with the dog behind.

Chapter Three

Ellen blinked.

No sign of the cat or dog. Not on the TV screen. Not in her living room. She shook her head. She must have imagined it.

She picked up the remote control and changed the channel to a baseball game.

"That's better," said Ellen and sat down to watch.

It was raining pretty hard, and the players were soaked, but still the game went on. The batter swung at the ball and *wham*!

Ellen ducked. The ball flew straight into her living room.

One of the outfielders jumped out of the TV and caught the ball, just before it hit the window.

"Hey," cried Ellen. "What're you doing in here?"

The outfielder cupped his hands to his face and hollered, "Come on, let's finish inside; at least it's dry."

All the players trooped out of the TV and into Ellen's living room. They were dripping wet and they tracked mud and grass all over the carpet.

Chapter Four

"Stop!" cried Ellen. "This is my house, not a baseball field. Get back in there."

"Nice place you got, kid," said the pitcher thumping her on the back.

Ellen gulped. She dived for the TV and turned it off.

But the players were still in her living room. They were moving the furniture out of the way.

"Maybe if I change channels, they'll disappear," thought Ellen. She turned on the TV and flicked channels.

"Oh no," she whispered.

The baseball players had started the game again — in her house.

CHAPTER FIVE

Just then, Ellen heard a yowl. The
cartoon cat and dog streaked around
the living room, tripping the players.

"Hey, kid," shouted the umpire. "Keep
your pets out of the game."

"They're not mine!" yelled Ellen.

"Time-out!" called the umpire.

The players groaned.

Someone cried out, "Let's get
something to eat."

Both teams tramped into the kitchen. They began opening the fridge and the cupboards, rooting around for food and drinks.

"Stop!" cried Ellen. "Mom and Dad will be awfully mad."

But the baseball players went on helping themselves.

Even the cat and dog snatched up ice-cream cones as they dashed by. The players carried their snacks back into the living room, laughing and joking.

"We're not allowed to eat in here," yelled Ellen to the umpire.

The umpire patted his stomach, burped and started the game again.

Chapter Six

Ellen groaned. "I'm in big trouble. If Mom and Dad see this mess, I'll be grounded forever."

She heard a roaring noise from the TV. There, on the screen, was a small, round man, with a huge vacuum cleaner.

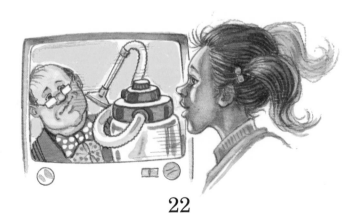

"Buy now," shouted the little man, in a surprisingly loud voice. "Honest Ollie's prices are rock bottom. This fantastic Suckeroo Vacuum Cleaner is only available at Honest Ollie's. Watch it in action."

Then before Ellen could say "Honest Ollie," the Suckeroo, followed by Honest Ollie, zoomed into her living room.

"No!" yelled Ellen. "We don't want any."

Honest Ollie flashed a big mouthful of teeth. "Of course you do, dear. Look at this place."

He rushed around the room cleaning up the mud and food. The cat shrieked and leaped onto the light fixture. It hung on with all ten claws, swinging wildly.

CHAPTER SEVEN

Ellen closed her eyes and wished with all her might, "Please, please, please, please, PLEASE. Make them get back in the box."

Ellen opened her eyes. Baseball players, mud, food, Honest Ollie, the cartoon cat and dog. Still there — in her living room.

Ellen took a deep breath and hollered as loudly as she could, "Listen here! This is MY house and I want all you to get out. RIGHT NOW!"

The first baseman took a huge bite of his baloney and banana sandwich. He said thickly, "Lighten up, kid. We're just having fun."

From behind her, Ellen heard the TV announcer, "Stay tuned folks. After this break we bring you Juanita's Wildlife Safari park. Wait 'til you see the famous lions!"

"Lions!" gulped Ellen. "I've got to do something. Fast."

CHAPTER SEVEN

Suddenly, Ellen had an idea.

She hid the remote control in her pocket and picked up her camera.

"Hey, everybody," shouted Ellen. "Can I take your picture?"

Faces turned to look at her. Honest Ollie turned off the Suckeroo.

Ellen put on her biggest, widest smile. "I've never met so many famous TV stars before. Please? It would mean an awful lot to me."

The baseball players grinned and shrugged. Honest Ollie slicked back his hair. Even the cartoon dog stopped barking, and popped on his sunglasses.

"Okay, let's take the picture in front of the TV," said Ellen.

Everyone crowded in front of the TV.

"Terrific," cried Ellen. "A little closer. Squeeze in."

Everyone smiled and hugged closer.

"Back some more," shouted Ellen. "More. A bit more."

They all shuffled backwards until they were standing just inside the TV set.

CHAPTER TEN

Ellen heard
the roar of lions.
She whipped out the
remote control from her
pocket and pressed the
off button.

The screen went blank and everyone
disappeared.

"Wow!" said Ellen. "That was close."

She took a deep breath and started to clean up.

Just as she finished Ellen's parents came inside. They looked dazed.

"I need to lie down," said her father, rubbing his eyes.

"What's wrong?" cried Ellen.

"We thought we saw a blue cartoon cat! Running into the house!"

Ellen's mother flopped into a chair. "It must be sunstroke. We'd better stay indoors."

"I wish that TV was working," sighed Ellen's father.

Ellen looked at her parents, the silent TV and the nice, quiet living room.

Slowly, she grinned. She handed her father the remote control.

"Try it, Dad. Maybe if we all wish really hard..."

FIRST FLIGHT®

*First Flight® is an exciting
new series of beginning readers.
The series presents titles which include songs,
poems, adventures, mysteries, and humour
by established authors and illustrators.
First Flight® makes the introduction to
reading fun and satisfying
for the young reader.*

*First Flight® is available in 4 levels
to correspond to reading development.*

Level 1 – Pre-school - Grade 1
Large type, repetition of simple concepts that are perfect
for reading aloud, easy vocabulary and endearing
characters in short simple stories for the earliest reader.

Level 2 – Grade 1 - Grade 3
Longer sentences, higher level of vocabulary, repetition,
and high-interest stories for the progressing reader.

Level 3 – Grade 2 - Grade 4
Simple stories with more involved plots and a simple
chapter format for the newly independent reader.

Level 4 – Grade 3 - up (First Flight Chapter Books)
More challenging level, minimal illustrations for the
independent reader.